G000065980

GAY ROMANCE COLLECTION VOLUME 2

CONNOR WHITELEY

No part of this book may be reproduced in any form or by any electronic or mechanical means. Including information storage, and retrieval systems, without written permission from the author except for the use of brief quotations in a book review.

This book is NOT legal, professional, medical, financial or any type of official advice.

Any questions about the book, rights licensing, or to contact the author, please email connorwhiteley@connorwhiteley.net

Copyright © 2021 CONNOR WHITELEY

All rights reserved.

DEDICATION

Thank you to all my readers without you I couldn't do what I love.

LOVE IN THE INGREDIENTS

Running his fingers gently over the smooth marble worktop of his kitchen, Sean took a deep breath of the cinnamon scented air, that reminded him of delicious apple pies as a kid, as he prepared himself for his next batch of cookies.

He was never normally this nervous about baking, he loved it, he loved the chemistry and the changes within the baked goods as they cooked and transformed into stunning perfection. But after the year him and his family had had, he just needed everything to go right.

As he felt the warmth from his black oven travel up his legs, he knew he had to get going on the next batch.

Looking at the silver bowl, teaspoons and spices in front of him, Sean sighed a little as he remembered why he was doing all of this. A part of him didn't want to bake yet another batch of cookies, he was sure if this was a normal time, then Sean knew he would have loved to bake even more.

But these were not normal times. At least not to him.

After his parents finding out he was gay in the January and all the loud moaning, screaming and unfriendliness that followed. Sean just wanted his dinner at Christmas to go well, his parents said they were sorry but he just wanted things to be okay.

Sean could hardly say that he wasn't surprised when his mum called up and asked if they could come round today for dinner.

At first Sean so badly wanted to say no, after everything they had put him through, Sean didn't want to see them. But he did love them, care about them and want to see them. So to his utter surprise he said yes.

The sound of cookies sizzling, cars driving past and the quiet Christmas songs in the background made Sean smile and push all those negative thoughts aside. This was going to be great, his parents and him were going to have an amazing dinner. But first he needed to make something special to go with coffee after dinner.

Even that memory of having coffee and something special after a grand meal made Sean relax a little, those times with his posh family were long gone (he wasn't invited anymore) but whilst the time lasted, it was great.

Returning his attention to the neatly arranged bowls, teaspoons and spices in front of him, Sean took out his phone and looked at the recipe.

It was a recipe for Brandy Snaps that one of his friends had sent him, Sean wasn't exactly sure if they were nice or if they were suitable for his parents' posh taste. They sounded posh but in Sean's experience that meant very, very little.

As he looked at the phone and the stupidly small text, Sean read that he needed butter, flour and sugar so he measured it and weight it all out.

With his strong arms mixing the butter and sugar together into a smooth paste before he added the flour, Sean knew this was going to be good. It was butter and sugar, what else did the dessert need?

For a moment, Sean remembered how his sister had actually had that in a sandwich before. Even now Sean hated the idea and found it completely disgusting, but he did love his sister. She was always a laugh. (At least from what Sean remembered)

After mixing that all together, Sean added the vanilla, milk and coffee. He mixed it all up for a few seconds and licked his lips.

Sean knew that if his parents didn't enjoy this then something was very wrong with them. They loved coffee, sweet things and vanilla. This was going to be the perfect thing to finish up a wonderful evening.

A part of Sean wondered if that last part was true, after everything that had happened, he didn't want tonight to be awkward or strange. He had a feeling (knew for a fact) that his father didn't want to come, it was just how he was. It was probably his mum that had arranged it all.

At least he might have one ally in case things go wrong. Sean relaxed a little at that idea, it was silly to feel like he needed allies but after the past year, very little surprised him anymore.

Returning his attention to his phone, he accidentally clicked off the recipe, so as he was trying to find it again. Sean wondered if he would be invited back to family events anytime soon. He wasn't really sure he cared that much, he was fine with being gay and he was more than happy.

It was everyone else that was the problem.

Sean smiled as he thought about the look on his family's face if he bought a boy back to them. Then he frowned as Sean remembered he had never had a boyfriend, he had always been too scared to get one. That needed to change.

After finding the recipe again, Sean looked at the last ingredient that he needed and rolled his eyes. He needed cream.

He didn't have any.

Taking a step away from the bowl of all the delicious ingredients and breathing in the coffee scented air, Sean wondered what to do next. He had to make these brandy snaps for his parents, he couldn't not make them, the fate of his relationship could be on the line.

Forcing himself to relax, Sean looked at the time and frowned when he saw it was four in the afternoon. His parents said they were coming at six, which in real life meant they were coming at half five. Sean didn't have time for this, but he had to make them. He had to find some cream.

As Sean remembered there was a shop within walking distance, he turned off the oven and put his mix in the fridge.

Then he dashed off, not knowing what he was going to find.

***

Hayden stared at his watch as he lent on the cold plastic till with sweets and scratch cards all around him as he waited for customers that were never going to turn up.

The cold air smelt of cigarette smoke from the awful smokers outside and Hayden hated the taste it formed in his mouth. But the sound of the smokers outside, the singing of Christmas Songs and the jolliness of little children running with their parents made him smile for a moment.

Then Hayden turned his attention back to his little shop with rows upon rows of food of all different types for people to buy.

It wasn't even his shop, it was his father's. A part of Hayden wondered why he bothered manning the shop for his father when his father could hire another young person who needed the money (and might actually enjoy it). During the week, Hayden loved being an office worker for his friend's company in insurance. But this customer-less shop was not what

Hayden wanted to do with his Saturday afternoon.

Looking back at his watch, Hayden rolled his eyes as it was only ten past 4, he wanted it to be five o'clock so he could go home and start decorating his Christmas tree in his little apartment.

He knew it would be more fun to have a boyfriend or someone else help him, but Hayden didn't have anyone yet. Normally his best friend came over and they would make a thing out of it, but she was away on business this weekend.

As Hayden listened to the smokers and everyone else walk away from outside the shop, he cocked his head as he wondered if he should just close up early. His father wouldn't mind and if he moaned about loss of earnings (which his father didn't need either), Hayden supposed he could give him some money.

Nodding to himself, Hayden was about to walk out from behind the counter when… wow! (Hayden almost swore)

Hayden's mouth dropped open when he saw an utterly stunning man about his age walk into the shop. The man's hair was beautifully long that seemed to flow down his shoulders like it was made from water.

This Man was fit with strong arm muscles and wearing his tight black coat and black jeans made him look even more stunning.

Hayden couldn't believe how amazing The Man looked. Somehow this Man even managed to make his skin look smooth, young and utterly amazing. But what really did it for Hayden was the Man's striking blue eyes.

The Man was perfection.

Hayden had to stop his thoughts from wondering what he would like to do to the Man's hair and his amazing body.

By this point, Hayden hadn't realised The Man had walked over to the till area with an equally massive smile. Hayden wanted to force himself to say something but he couldn't The Man was so beautiful and that's all he could focus on.

It was that moment Hayden knew he was going to be in trouble (or maybe love).

***

Breathing in the horrible smoke from the smokers standing outside the shop, Sean waved at them as they started to sing Christmas songs at him. But Sean couldn't really understand the image of Christmas singers smoking, the two didn't seem to connect in his mind.

With Sean knowing he had to get some cream no matter what, he watched the smokers put out their cigarettes and walk down the street singing their Christmas songs loudly and he entered the shop.

When he walked into the shop, Sean ignored the rows upon rows of great looking foods and all the other essentials that people would need and didn't want to go to a supermarket for. Instead Sean knew it was best to just ask the person at the till.

As he looked around for the till, Sean felt the cold wrap around him and he was instantly glad he hadn't done what he normally did, and take off his coat as soon as he walked in anywhere.

For a few moments of looking, Sean found the till and the amazing smell of strong aftershave filled the air as Sean looked at the-

Sean didn't know what to think or say or do as he stared into the drop-dead gorgeous eyes of the guy at the till. He was definitely Sean's age with an amazing slim body and short blond hair.

But what really, really, really did it for Sean was the guy's face. It was squarish but it was perfectly smooth and it was perfectly framed by his eyes and hairs with a strong jawline.

The Guy looked like some sort of movie star, he shouldn't have been working in some shop. He should be working on film sets, sweeping up women (and hopefully men) and enjoying being a movie star.

Sean instantly felt bad as he never ever acted like this, whenever he normally saw a guy he liked. He would try and ignore his feelings or he would just suppress them and never act on them. Actually being attracted and thinking like this towards the Till Guy was strange.

But it felt so good to him.

Remembering why he was there (and trying to stop his wayward parts from doing things), Sean walked up to the Till Guy. Partly because he needed cream, partly because Sean had to talk to Till Guy.

But when he got to the till, Sean couldn't stop smiling as he breathed in more of the Till Guy's stunning aftershave and looked deeper into his amazing eyes.

Sean knew he had to talk so he just went for it.

"I need cream. Parents hate me. I'm gay. I need to create a nice dish. They're coming tonight. I need cream!"

As soon as he finished Sean wanted to run out of the shop and never return, but to his (utter) surprise the Till Guy smiled even more and looked to take a few deep breaths.

Sean took a few deep breaths of his own.

"I'm sorry about I know I must have sounded strange. Do you have any cream please?" Sean asked.

"Yes it's in the back next to the milk. And if it helps, it's okay. I don't know about family not taking it well, but I do understand it," the Till Guy said.

For some reason, Sean relaxed and felt a weight he didn't even know he was holding. He had always thought he was okay with what had happened, but he supposed it was nice to hear he wasn't alone in people not liking him.

"Friends?" Sean asked.

The Till Guy nodded.

"I'm sorry to hear that. I'm Sean,"

Sean's eyes narrowed on the Till Guy as he seemed to smile and bite his lip at hearing his name. He wasn't exactly sure how to act, Sean had never had this happen to him before.

"I'm Hayden," Till Guy said.

Now Sean wanted to kick himself as he noticed

he had bit his own lip. Hayden was a hot name. Hell, Hayden was hot!

In some bad attempt to stop himself from doing something foolish, Sean walked to the back of the shop and grabbed a large cold bottle of cream.

"Why are your parents coming tonight?" Hayden asked.

Sean opened his mouth, but he realised he really didn't know.

"I'm sorry. That was probably too personal," Hayden said.

"No it's fine. I just don't know. I just… want it to go well," Sean said, feeling a bit light-headed as Hayden smiled at him once more.

"Have you got a friend going with you?" Hayden asked.

Sean's eyebrows rose. He had no idea why he needed to have a friend, he had hoped everything would be fine without anyone else, but what if Hayden knew something Sean didn't?

"Sorry. I remember when some of my friends wanted to come back. I felt like it helped me to have my bestie with me," Hayden said.

Sean's eyes narrowed. It wasn't a bad idea and he had thought about having allies earlier, maybe this would be a good idea. But who could he call this late on a Saturday afternoon?

Sean wondered what his best friend was doing but he was probably busy with his own boyfriend, his other friends probably had Christmas plans this weekend and… he didn't have anyone else.

The amazing smell of Hayden's strong aftershave made Sean smile as he decided he had to do something crazy.

"Do you want to come?" Sean quickly asked.

As soon as he said it, he felt like an idiot, he had only just met Hayden and he was basically asking him out on a date. He couldn't do that, could he?

Sean just wanted to run out the shop.

But to his surprise, Hayden looked a little flushed.

"Yes," Hayden said, sounding as unsure as Sean.

Sean didn't exactly know what to do so he smiled and pretended to act natural (and completely trying not to panic inside!).

"Great, parents coming at half five. Dinner for six," Sean said failing to sound cool.

Then Sean saw the time on Hayden's watch and his eyes widened. It was half four. He had to go.

He got out his wallet but Hayden touched his hand softly. Sean couldn't help but smile at the pure power flowing between them. he loved it. He loved the feeling. He wanted more.

"Sean, it's fine. I'll pay,"

Sean nodded and gave Hayden a boyish grin as he left the shop, looking forward to dinner for an entirely new reason now.

***

As he watched the shop door close, Hayden's eyes widened as he just realised what he'd done.

Breathing in the cold air with hints of smoke from those smokers earlier, Hayden looked around at all the rows upon rows of food and other essentials. He didn't know what he was looking for but he hoped to find something.

In all honesty, Hayden guessed he was probably looking for a nice bottle of wine or something to take to his new dinner host.

The sound of Christmas songs and cars driving past quietly filled the air as Hayden slowly walked past the shelves of food to the back of the shop where the wine was kept.

A part of Hayden wanted to kick himself for what he just agreed to. Whenever he was normally around boys he was calm, collective and he would never ever agree to go on a random dinner date with a hot man he only just met.

But Sean was special.

Hayden rolled his eyes as he knew he sounded like some loved up person, but he really believed it. He loved Sean's amazing long hair, eyes and his stunning strong arms.

It still didn't make Hayden feel any better, he still felt like he was intruding in something important and something that was nothing to do with him.

But it was.

As Hayden remembered how much support his best friend had given him during his own dinner with friends that had called him awful things. Hayden didn't want to tell Sean that it would be awkward at times and maybe it would go badly.

Then Hayden remembered that it was his best friend that had supported him and made sure it went smoothly as possible. Hayden had always loved his best friend for that.

Yet Sean didn't have anyone like that available.

When he got to the end of the shop, Hayden stared at all the black, clear and even red bottles of wine that were neatly arranged in tall rows on the shelf in front of him. The fridge behind the shelf hummed along to itself and Hayden ran his fingers across the cold glass of the bottles.

Hayden felt his hand shake a little as he looked over and over the wine labels as if his life depended on choosing the right bottle for the dinner. He knew he was being silly but he supposed he wanted, no needed this to go right. He needed Sean to like him but most of all Hayden needed to be there to support Sean.

When his fingers were starting to turn a little numb from the cold glass of all the wine, Hayden touch the label of an expensive red wine from France. It was one of the more expensive ones in the shop but for some reason it felt right.

Hayden looked at the price tag and he surprised even himself. The wine was definitely way over £10, a price he would never consider buying before, but on this occasion it felt right. It felt okay. It felt… good.

Picking up the cold bottle of red wine, Hayden looked around the shop and saw it was completely empty like it was before. There was no one coming, no more customers, no more money coming in today.

Everyone was out living their lives.

So Hayden knew he had to do the same, he had to pay for the cream and wine, go home, get changed and go and support an utterly stunning man.

***

After whipping up the cream with vanilla and sugar added to it, Sean took a deep breath of the stew scented air with other hints of sweet desserts mixed into it too. Sean loved the smell, it was so welcoming, so inviting, so relaxing.

The last one might have been wishful thinking but Sean hoped not. He really, really wanted this all to go perfectly.

As he popped the cream in the fridge for later, Sean pressed his back against the cold grey fridge and took a few more deep breaths. He wasn't relaxed, he knew that but he didn't know why.

He knew tonight was tense and it could go wrong in a million different ways, but Sean knew he was okay on that front. He had made amazing food, even got his parents a present or two each and he had… he had a support person.

Just the reminder of what he had dragged Hayden into made Sean accidentally bang the back of his head against the bridge.

A part of Sean didn't know why he invited a complete stranger into his life like that and more importantly to a dinner with his parents. He supposed he didn't need another factor to annoy his parents. What if his parents didn't like Hayden?

Why did it matter?

Sean cocked his head as he remembered that question from his best friend soon after his parents had said awful things to him. He didn't know why it mattered, but it did. Sean loved his parents, he wanted them in his life, he wanted to be accepted.

But then Sean realised no matter what happened tonight, if Hayden turned up then everything was going to be okay. Hayden was a super hot guy that Sean wanted, needed to be with. Hayden was hot, kind and Sean knew he would be perfect boyfriend material.

Then his stomach churned as Sean wondered what if he was the problem. Sean had never had a boyfriend before, he didn't know what to do, how to date, he-

The sound of a knock on the door made Sean tense then relax as he looked at the time and it was before half five.

It was Hayden. He had actually come.

Sean felt his hands go sweaty as he realised that Hayden actually cared about him. Sean had never known a man to care about him before. Maybe this could work out, maybe tonight was going to be great, maybe-

The sound of the door knocking got louder and Sean smiled as he walked through his house to the door and opened it.

His smile deepened as he looked into the striking blue eyes and stunning movie star face of Hayden. Sean placed his hand on the doorframe and couldn't help but stare at the stunning man in front of him.

Hayden placed his hand on the doorframe too and they both smiled like schoolboys as their fingers touched each other. And it was then that Sean changed his mind about the entire evening, he really didn't care about what happened, because he had Hayden and he hoped that this was going to last a very long time.

And this all happened because of some ingredients.

PARTY, LOVE, CHRISTMAS

With the quiet stand mixer humming and mixing in the background and the sound of the quiet Christmas songs playing too, Percy stared wide eyed at all the streaks of cake batter, sprinkles and flour everywhere. Percy just stared at the beautiful mess in the kitchen. He wasn't sure why he thought it was beautiful, but Percy hoped this mess was going to lead to something magical.

As he stared at the beautiful mess, he shook his head as he breathed in the heavenly scent of the sponges baking in the oven, already for him and his best friend Megan to decorate and assemble for the Christmas party tonight.

Percy could already taste the amazing vanilla and chocolate sponge in his mouth, it was going to be amazing. At least all the baking stopped Percy from worrying for a few moments about the party.

The party wasn't anything grand, it was a normal Christmas party with all the friends and colleagues from his new job in Megan's office. But that didn't make Percy feel any better, he had barely been there a week, and now he had to go to a party!

Trying to push those thoughts away, Percy returned his attention to the messy kitchen and he went to grab a tea towel to wipe it up before he heard light footsteps and Megan, who wore her normal black jeans, loose blue shirt and tennis shoes, pop back into the kitchen.

With Megan slipping past him and returning to her work in the kitchen like there was no mess at all, Percy shook his head and looked at her. Wondering how long it would take her to notice the mess was there.

Granted knowing Megan, she would probably say it wasn't a mess but a part of the baking experience. Percy didn't have the heart to tell her, it was the part of the baking experience *with her*.

As much as Percy loved to cook, create things and give them to people as gifts. He never got this messy and as he took a step towards Megan, he felt flour and wet cake batter under his feet.

"Come on Pers," Megan said. "Need that recipe,"

He had no idea what there was left to make, they had already made sponges, sandwiches and Swiss rolls for the Christmas party. Percy didn't think they needed anymore but Megan always wanted to make her famous (only to her) mini-Christmas puddings, and Percy had learnt a long time ago never to upset

Megan.

As he got out his large black phone and flickered through it, Percy remembered how he had watched plenty of (hot) men go against Megan's wishes before and that never went down well.

Percy never understood why Megan was so stubborn but he had learnt to live and even love it a little.

"Come on Pers! They're waiting for my famous Christmas Puddings!" Megan shouted.

Percy smiled. "Yea, yea,"

After a few more moments of looking, he found the recipe she had sent him.

"Found it Meg,"

"Good. Read out the ingredients to me,"

"Including weights?"

"Heavens no Pers. My famous recipe is wonderful, I've made it so many times. I know it like the back of my hands,"

Again Percy didn't have the heart to tell her that her Christmas Puddings were not wonderful. He almost laughed as he remembered all the times him and his friends had had to secretly bin the puddings.

"Your basic mix, treacle and brandy," Percy said.

For a moment, Percy wondered what she meant by basic mix but when he saw her add flour, butter and sugar to the large silver mixing bowl, he understood. He just hoped these tasted good.

"Know who's coming tonight?" Megan asked.

"Of course not. I only know the people from

HR. They don't go to parties!" Percy said, remembering how depressing his first two days were in HR. He had no idea how much paperwork and health and safety training was involved in his job.

"True," Megan said sounding like she was trying not to laugh.

"Who's going then?"

Megan clicked her fingers and Percy looked back at his phone.

"You need cinnamon, cloves, brandy and golden syrup," Percy said. Maybe these would be good with a bit of golden syrup in them.

"These will be the best puddings ever. Far better than Missy's puddings,"

Percy raised his hand to his forehead as he now understood why Megan wanted to go to the party for the first time. In all the past five years Megan had worked there, Percy had never heard of her wanting to go, most weekends' before Christmas him and Megan finished the Christmas shopping, bought presents for each other and their boyfriends and occasionally went out for dinner.

But now Percy was starting to get why she *had* to go this year.

"Who's Missy?" Percy asked.

Megan turned towards Percy. "You know Pers. That woman who flirts with the boss and gets to leave an hour before me!"

Percy shrugged.

"Stick woman!"

Percy shook his head smiling. He loved the nicknames she gave her friends, peers and basically everyone she met. Percy didn't want to know his.

"There's plenty of boys for you tonight," Megan said. Quickly turning back to the mixture.

Percy looked at her. "Is that what this is about? You want me to hook up with someone,"

"No," Megan said unconvincingly.

"I don't-"

"Pers I love you, but you don't have a boyfriend. You haven't had one for ages and this Christmas party is perfect for meeting new people. Even if you don't meet a boyfriend or hook up, at least try and meet some new people,"

Percy shook his head and knew she was right, he did need to meet some new people and get to know his work friends better.

"Fine,"

"Brillant. Now pass me the salt please,"

As he passed Megan the salt to apparently add a contrast to all the sugar, Percy didn't know whether he was going to find new friends, or save everyone from these puddings!

***

Patrick loved Christmas parties. They were the best things ever to be invented. Even tonight the Christmas songs were playing loudly in the large open plan office and everyone was having fun.

Pressing his strong muscular back against the cold wall of the office, Patrick looked out over the large office that was now a dance floor with men and women of all different ages and sizes dancing along to whatever song was blasting itself.

At the moment it was *Santa Claus Is Coming To Town*, Patrick loved this song but he loved all of the songs, he just loved Christmas. It was such a magical time of year that was full of amazing people, presents and miracles.

Of course it was better to share it with someone but Patrick knew he would find someone eventually. A small part of him hoped he would find someone tonight, he did believe in Christmas miracles after all, but he was going to enjoy the party no matter what.

The smell of all the cakes, sandwiches, sausage rolls and the rest of the things that people bought in a hurry at the local shop before coming to the party.

Patrick had almost forgotten himself that he needed to bring food and some drink for the party so he quickly dashed into a Marks & Spencers and bought a few things without looking. (He knew he'd regret it when he checked his bank account tomorrow!)

With the smell of the amazing food washing over the room, in addition to all the other hints and scents from people's perfumes and aftershaves, Patrick couldn't stop smiling as he soaked in all the amazing vibes of the party.

There wasn't a single person frowning or being sad. Everyone was happy, alive and partying. Even the people from HR were dancing!

If that didn't confirm Christmas miracles were real, then nothing would.

As the song changed to *Santa Baby*, Patrick checked his expensive gold watch and wondered when Megan was going to turn up. Patrick didn't want to see her famous (famous for the wrong reasons) Christmas Puddings, but he did want to see her. She was always a laugh and fun to be around.

Megan had said that she was bringing a friend that Patrick would like to the party, but from past experience, Patrick knew that meant very little. Megan was friends with the best people on the planet to some of the less good people and everyone in between.

For all Patrick knew this friend would be a paper pusher for the government or a fireman. Patrick smiled at the last idea, he definitely wouldn't mind Megan bringing a fireman to the party.

Noticing there was a little less dancing, Patrick returned his attention to the middle of the office and saw some people were opening the massive glass doors to let two people walk in.

Patrick instantly smiled when he saw Megan in her long black dress and holding god knows how many containers of food. He really hoped she didn't bring the Christmas puddings.

Then Patrick's eyes narrowed on the other new person he hadn't seen before and… wow!

As Patrick stared at the amazing man at Megan's side, his mouth dropped open a little bit and he felt sweat drip off his palms and back.

Patrick couldn't believe how amazing this Mystery Man looked with his tight black shirt, dark brown eyes and stunning cheekbones. He looked amazing, perfect even.

The more he stared, the more Patrick felt his cheeks warm up and he knew he had to talk to this Mystery Guy. He was stunning, and tall!

So Patrick pushed himself off the wall and went over to talk to this amazing, perfectly beautiful Mystery Guy in case this would be another Christmas miracle.

***

Walking along the massive white corridor, passing pictures and other offices, Percy definitely understood now why he was bought along. He was certain all that stuff about Missy and Megan wanting him to find a boyfriend was all just a smoke screen.

Megan just wanted the help for her food.

Percy could hear the Christmas songs playing from here and all that hopefulness and joy was hardly helping him right now as he held container after container of party food for Megan.

Granted she was holding tons too (which surprised Percy) so they were both struggling up the corridor. But the food did smell great, Percy loved the smell of the light sponges, sweet Christmas puddings and all the other food Megan had cooked in his kitchen.

After a few more moments of struggling, Percy

rolled his eyes as he saw two large glass doors to their office but they were closed.

"Guys, food!" Megan shouted.

And if by magic (or everyone knowing how stubborn and bossy Megan was), the door opened and they went inside.

Percy was struggling with all the containers too much to focus on the large office and everyone in the middle dancing as he followed Megan towards the food table. He set the containers on the floor and passed them to Megan in her black dress (that made some straight guys stare at her).

"Isn't this wonderful?" Megan said, sounding more and more excited by the minute.

Percy wished he could share her excitement but he had just struggled to move containers full of amazing food from his car, up tens of flights of stairs (because lifts would spoil the food apparently) and along the corridor. Percy would love to meet anyone who could stay Christmas-y after all that. So Percy knew it would take him a little while to get his Christmas spirit back after all that.

But as he listened to the Christmas songs, saw all the people enjoying the party and breathing in the delicious smell of the food, Percy supposed it wouldn't take long.

"Pers pass me-" Megan said as Percy passed her the (horrible) Christmas puddings.

Percy knelt down to pick up the last of the doomed Christmas puddings and when he stood out up he never expected to see the gorgeous man standing in front of him.

Percy's eyes instantly widened as he stared at the round little face with dark green eyes and short ginger hair. Percy had never known himself to be into red haired men before, but Mr gorgeous definitely convinced him otherwise.

Before he knew it, Percy had quickly looked the gorgeous man up and down. Admiring the man's shiny black shoes, tight trousers and his tight baby blue shirt that was hiding a ripped body underneath.

Mr Gorgeous was just that. Gorgeous.

Percy felt like he wanted to speak but his mind went blank and he only wanted to focus on the beautiful man in front of him. He didn't want to focus on Christmas songs, the other people or even the container of horrible Christmas puddings in his hand.

He only wanted to look at Mr Gorgeous.

"Pers! Pass me the last puds please," Megan said. Making Percy instantly come out of his trance and pass the container over to Megan.

As soon as he had given Megan the container, Percy looked into Mr Gorgeous' amazing dark green eyes and found the courage to talk to him.

"Hi," Percy said before his mouth went dry and again he got lost in Mr Gorgeous' dark eyes.

"Hey I'm Patrick," Mr Gorgeous said holding out his hand.

"Percy," he said as he shook *Patrick's* hand slowly

and he noticed they were both gently rubbing each other's hands like it was the last time they would ever touch. Percy didn't want that, he wanted to touch a lot more, but a simple handshake would have to be enough. He loved the feeling of his skin tingle and the electricity flow between them as they touched for the first, but hopefully not the last time.

"Pers you found Patty. Brilliant!" Megan said as she squeezed past the two men before disappearing into the crowd of dancing people who were now dancing to *Rocking Around The Christmas Tree.*

"Please tell me she didn't bring her puddings," Patrick asked.

Percy smiled. "Sadly. I wanted to bin them. Sorry,"

"No problem. I always let my dogs eat them,"

Percy's eyes narrowed on gorgeous Patrick, he did like dogs and animal lovers, especially red hair animals lovers, were hot. Percy kept taking steps forwards until him and Patrick were slightly away from the food table, so they could talk a little more without possible Megan interruptions.

"What kinds?" Percy asked. In reality he had no idea about dogs, he wouldn't have known a Jack Russel from a bulldog, but this gorgeous man was interesting and Percy didn't want to stop talking to him.

"Two bulldogs and a Yorkshire terrier," Patrick said. "Want to see them?"

As much as Percy wanted him to mean take him

back to his place and show him, Percy sadly knew what he meant so Percy nodded. And instantly wanted to kick him for acting or having such a dirty thought after just meeting the man. He wanted to know why he was acting like this but he was scared he already knew the answer.

When Patrick got out his phone, he showed Percy photos of the cute dogs and Percy loved feeling Patrick's body warmth when he *accidentally* pressed himself against him.

Patrick didn't back away.

Normally Percy would have cursed or panicked whenever he even wondered about doing this to a hot man, but being so close to Patrick felt so natural, even good, even perfect.

"Pers!" Megan shouted from across the dance floor and waving him over.

Percy frowned and looked a couple of times between Megan and Patrick before knowing he should probably go and see what she wanted.

He looked back at gorgeous Patrick, wishing this moment would never end.

"I'm sorry she needs me,"

Patrick gave Percy a sad smile. "It's okay. I'm not going anywhere,"

Percy wanted to think about his words and saviour them but Megan shouted his name again.

But he hoped, prayed, whatever that Patrick wasn't going anywhere.

***

As he watched that utterly stunning man walk off through the dance floor as they were literally *Rocking Around The Christmas Tree*, Patrick felt his heart drop as he realised that that magical moment of chemistry and staring into those amazing eyes was over.

Patrick breathed in the amazing smells of the food mixed in with the scents and hints of the strong aftershaves and perfumes of the other people, and he pressed his back against the warm wall next to the massive food table.

He supposed he should go into the dance floor and join in all the fun but for the first time ever in the history of his Christmas parties, he didn't feel like it. He didn't want to move, he didn't want to eat or dance. He just wanted to stay here where that stunningly beautiful Percy could find him.

Patrick wanted to laugh at himself because out of all his past boyfriends and even a few girls when he was straight, he had never felt like this. He felt like he had just met the most amazing person ever and now they were gone.

Patrick knew it didn't make sense but he had felt the power, electricity and chemistry between him and Percy. He wanted that feeling again and again and again so it would never end.

As Patrick looked across the dance floor, listened to the Christmas songs playing and breathed in the amazing smell of the food, Patrick knew that he was really wasn't going anywhere. He would wait, try some of the horrible Christmas puddings and wait just in case Percy came back to him.

Whether it was for the rest of the night or just longer, Patrick would wait. Just in case it was a Christmas miracle.

***

After gliding his way through the crowd of people enjoying themselves on the dance floor, dancing, drinking and eating. The air was starting to smell of sweat with hints of the perfume and aftershave from the dancing people, but Percy saw Megan in her black dress talking to a tall attractive man in a black suit as she sipped her cocktail.

"What's up Meg?" Percy asked.

"Pers. What's going on with my famous puddings?"

Percy tried not to frown at her. He had been loving his moment with Patrick and she disturbed him for some news about her horrible puddings.

"No one's tried them," Percy said.

"No! Oh my god, people don't know what they're missing. They're perfect,"

Percy gave a sideward glance to the other man and he shrugged. Everyone in the office knew not to touch Megan's puddings.

"Daniel you have to try a pudding," Megan said to the other man.

"Sorry Meggy, I think my wife's calling me," the other man said as he rushed off holding his turned off phone to his ear.

"Pers I'm starting to think people don't like my

puddings,"

Percy hugged her. "Megan,"

As Percy released her from the hug, he breathed in her flowery perfume and looked gently into her large brown eyes.

"What's wrong Pers?"

"You know we all love you but your puddings… they're awful,"

Percy was expecting for some grand argument why they're the best things ever but he was surprised when he saw her nodding and look to the floor.

"Pers. I… I just wanted people to like me and I need to be helpful,"

Percy laughed a little. "Meg, everyone here loves you. Everyone thinks you're amazing and you really interrupted me with Patrick,"

He was expecting to say the last part but now he had said it Percy was going with it.

Megan cocked her head, her eyes narrowing on Percy.

"Really Pers? You were only talking,"

Percy shook his head. "Yes but… he's a great guy. He's hot, beautiful and kind. I…"

As he trailed off, Percy realised he really cared about Patrick, he had come here tonight looking for new friends and maybe a boyfriend (but mainly as muscle for Megan's food containers).

Yet as Percy looked at Megan and saw her infectious smile, he knew he hadn't found a friend, a boyfriend, he had found something a lot more precious.

A soul mate.

A person to spend Christmas with, laugh with and love with. Percy couldn't believe he was thinking this, he hadn't thought about anyone like this before, but he was being honest with himself. Something he rarely did.

And he really wanted Patrick. Hopefully not just for the night, Christmas but hopefully a lot longer.

Megan placed a gentle warm hand on Percy's cheek.

"You're wrong about my puddings. But go and be with Patrick,"

"Really?"

"Yes. I'll get Daniel to drive me home,"

Percy was about to thank her before Megan rushed off into the dancing crowd in the middle of the office.

"Daniel!" Megan shouted.

A tiny part of Percy didn't know what he had just inflicted onto poor Daniel, but none of that mattered. As Percy breathed in the warm air with all the hints of perfume, aftershave and food. He looked across the dance floor and saw the most amazing sight imaginable.

He saw Patrick staring straight at him, smiling and waiting. Percy felt a wave of pure excitement travel up his spine and into his head (and wayward organs) as he felt surprised that this gorgeous stunning man had waited for him.

Percy glided through the crowd and saw Patrick walk towards him, and Percy knew that this was going to be a great Christmas and hopefully a lot, lot longer.

GAY, LOVE, HEIR

Feeling the cold wintery air brush over his cheeks as the wind blew gently, Stan kept walking up the long concrete path running up the hill to the university. Beautiful bright green trees lined the path and the sound of other students walking, talking and even cycling up and down filled the air as Stan kept walking.

He had one of his favourite classes that he wasn't going to miss for the world, he loved his biological psychology lectures. Stan just thought it was amazing how our biology could impact our behaviour in so many breath-taking ways. So he kept walking, he didn't want to be late.

As he walked he listened to the brief conversations of other students, they were all so glad to be back after the Christmas holidays, it was great to be back studying, learning and most importantly seeing friends.

That was something that Stan's parents never

quite understood about why he was excited to be back. He really wanted to catch up with his French and Spanish friends that had travelled back home for Christmas.

The smell of aftershaves made Stan smile a little as he saw some hot guys walk past as they left for the day. Stan supposed they were lucky with only having one lecture at the crack of dawn (9 am) but Stan still loved his midday lecture and then the rest in the afternoon.

When he neared the top of the hill, the path continued into the university grounds along wide open fields of lush green grass and Stan was filled with a sense of relief. He was back and he in a strange way, he was home. University had always been a home away from home for Stan, a home for learning, making friendships and maybe even finding love.

Stan's smile thinned a little as he wondered about finding love. Being gay at a university didn't sound hard in the slightest and he knew how fortunate he was to have the full support of his entire family (sometimes a little too much support!) but it didn't mean finding other gay people was easy.

Pushing those thoughts away, Stan continued to walk along the long concrete path that breathe in the fresh wintery air as the gentle wind flew past, and he continued to be more relaxed as he was back at university.

The place he belonged.

Knowing he had ages (tens of metres) to go

before he actually reached the university campus and even then it was a trek and a half to get to where his lecture was, Stan wondered what new students there would be today.

Even being in his first year at university Stan had made friends with some older students for hook-ups and apparently on the first day of the spring term (which Stan never quite understood because it was still January) new students would always turn up. Regardless of them being new domestic students or new foreign exchange students.

For some reason Stan felt his stomach fill with butterflies of meeting new people and potentially meeting new men. He smiled to himself as he knew at silly he was being. He studied psychology, human behaviour which was a female course mainly.

Stan's smile deepened as he remembered the jokes from his family about it was a shame he wasn't straight with all those women and it makes sense a gay should want to do what women do.

Stan still couldn't believe that they actually said about that but he agreed it was funny, and he did laugh.

But with psychology being a female-dominated course, it was rubbish for gay people. Stan never ever said that but he did think it. And to make things even worse, the men that were on the course were either straight or too straight acting to tell, and Stan had learnt long, long ago you never ask a man straight away if they were gay or not.

Still Stan really couldn't believe how silly his young self was.

But as he walked onto the university campus with the tall metal buildings around him, the air a strange mix of weed and fresh wintery air, Stan took a deep breath (coughed at the weed) and knew it was great to be back.

And this was going to be a great day. He just didn't know why.

***

With the sound of hundreds of students in all their different classes, heights and sizes talking, laughing and shouting around him, Robert pressed himself into a little corner of the white walled corridor as he waited for the lecture doors to open so he could go into his first lecture as an official university student.

Well, he had been a student at another place but… that didn't end up so well. So he came here to Canterbury, England and he hoped (he really, really hoped) things would work out better.

Breathing in the smell of expensive perfumes, aftershaves and some fresh air from the open windows, Robert looked down on the corridor and just couldn't believe how many students were here.

At his last university he was lucky to have another hundred or two in joined him in a lecture, but this was a lot more. It was easily three or four hundred students. Robert wasn't sure why the university designed this lecture theatre to be only accessed by a small corridor that was never ever going to fit hundreds of students at any one point.

Pushing those thoughts away, Robert pressed himself even tighter against the cold white wall as more students tried to pack themselves into the corridor. Robert wasn't a fan of the cold wall chill his back, he just hoped not all lectures were like this.

He didn't want a repeat of his last time, he just wanted a fresh start. A chance to make new friends, learning and maybe escape his life in the arms of a beautiful man.

Robert caught a laugh that almost escaped as he knew the last part was impossible. He was gay and proud and happy, but it seemed his happiness didn't matter, at least not in the eyes of his parents and wider family.

Robert rested his head against the cold wall allowing, willing the cold to chill his head as he remembered how he met a beautiful man at his last university and he was truly in love. He really loved that man. But his parents found out.

Robert bit his lip and frowned as he remembered how annoyed they were and how they threatened to cut him off and abandon him if Robert didn't change universities.

Listening to the sounds of more talking, laughing and shouting from his fellow students, Robert just stood there. He didn't want to think about the past, he wanted to learn and escape his home life, get a great job so he would never have to depend on his parents.

But his eyes wetted.

For some reason Robert knew that future was a long, long time away, and he hated how much longer he would have to deny himself what he loved and wanted to have fun experiencing.

Robert lifted up his head as he saw the massive group of students moving as it looked like someone or maybe more than one person was coming through the crowd. Robert leant forward as he wanted this to be the lecturer so he could get on with learning and forget about all his troubles.

But it wasn't.

It was just a group of students. Robert was about to look away when... his mouth dropped as he looked at the most beautiful man he had ever seen.

The Guy's beauty was staggering, it wasn't natural. Robert knew he was probably being silly but this Guy was... stunningly perfect.

Robert loved the Guy's tall slim body, sapphire eyes and his movie star smile. He was staggering, beautiful, perfect even. Robert quickly forgets all about his home life as he stared at this Guy with his staggering beauty.

***

When Stan turned the corner, he shook his head as he stared wide-eyed at all the students in all their different heights, classes and sizes who were just rammed into the little white walled corridor.

There was no reason for it but Stan was glad he

was still slightly early, he didn't even want to imagine what this crowd of students would be like if all four hundred students had turned up.

Normally Stan was early so he always missed these pre-lecture crams, but this was his first day back and clearly all the Christmas drinks and food had made him forget what university was like.

The smell of perfume from all the women was a little overpowering and it made the taste of faint chemicals form on his tongue, but Stan liked the smell, he really did. They were some great scents here and a part of Stan wondered if it would be weird to ask them what they were. He knew he couldn't tell them the perfume would be for him but he could just lie. The last thing he wanted was a rumour going round campus that he was really into perfumes and all the stereotypical gay things.

Forgetting about the perfume, Stan felt the cold air blow past him from the open glass windows and he looked at the crowd of students. He needed to get to the front to ask a question to the lecturer, he supposed he could talk to the lecturer after the lecture. But the Christmas drinks and food didn't fade the memory of how impossible that was after the talk as that's when everyone wanted to ask questions.

Stan knew he had to try another way.

As he focused on the massive crowd of students, Stan noticed there was a slight gap along the corridor where the full coldness of the windows would be felt. That was probably why no one was standing there yet.

Stan went for it.

He slowly glided through the massive crowd of students, his back cold as it touched the glass, and his nose filled the scents of perfume. Stan wanted to shake his head as he noticed a few students were following him as they all glided between the crowd and the cold windows.

After a few moments, Stan got to the front of the crowd and smiled to himself that he had finally got to the front. Now he could ask his question to the-

Stan's entire mind stopped as he looked at the only man in front of him. Stan's mind went blank as he stared at the beautiful man.

Stan couldn't quite understand what was so special or beautiful about the man, but he just was. Stan supposed it could have been the man's thin but strong jawline, bright seductive green eyes and longish blond hair. But this man was just beautiful.

Stan felt his palms turn sweaty and before he knew it he had walked over and he was standing just in front of the beautiful man in the little corner. Stan knew he had to say something but the man was still too beautiful and Stan's mind was still blank.

"Hi," the beautiful man said, sounding just as weak as Stan.

Stan's smile deepened as he listened to the man's smooth voice.

"I'm Robert," the man said.

Robert. Now that was a hot name.

Then Stan noticed that *Robert's* eyes were

gesturing him to speak, and Stan realised that he needed to introduce himself. It annoyed him a little how his mind wasn't working today.

"Hey I'm Stan,"

Stan instantly regretted his name as he realised how lame it must have sounded. It was nowhere near as hot and sexy as Robert. Stan just sounded silly.

But just as if Robert had read his mind, he said:

"That's a good name," he said biting his lip.

"Thanks, you new?" Stan asked.

"Yea I was at… another place before. I just got here today. It's ma first day,"

Stan's eyes narrowed a little. He could hear the sadness and regret in Robert's voice, he didn't like hearing or seeing this beautiful man in any sort of pain. Stan wanted to give him a hug or provide some sort of (physical) comfort to him but Stan knew that wasn't appropriate. Was it?

"I'm sorry," Robert said.

Stan really wanted to kick himself now. He wish he wasn't this easy to read, he didn't want Robert to think he was pitying or seeing him as someone to be cared for.

Stan opened his mouth but he didn't know what to say. Then he just decided to go with the classics.

"You okay?"

For a moment Stan didn't know if Robert was going to answer because he still stared at Stan, his eyes soft and… even longing for something that Stan didn't know. Maybe a friend, maybe someone to talk to, maybe something more.

The sound of the students falling silent and shuffling made Stan and Robert turn to see the lecturer coming down the hall and the lecture was going to begin soon.

Stan knew he had to offer something to Robert. He didn't know why, he didn't know why he was acting like this, but it didn't change how he felt.

"I'm going to library afterwards if you want someone to talk to," Stan said as the lecture opened the door and everyone went inside.

***

Sitting in the soft fold up chairs that were arranged level upon level like an amphitheatre in the lecture theatre, Robert stared at the PowerPoint that was on the large screen covering the wall in front of him.

He stared at it but he wasn't focusing on it, the PowerPoint was looking at the impact of hormones on behaviour and Robert couldn't concentrate enough to look at it.

As he felt the soft material of the chair between his fingers, breathed in the perfume and air conditioned scents and listened to the lecturer give a passionate talk about the topic, Robert couldn't stop thinking about Stan.

Robert was sure Stan didn't like his own name but he did. Stan was the sort of name that belonged to a manly man, a practical man, a hot man. Which Stan definitely was. Robert remembered Stan's staggering beauty and how badly he wanted to be with him.

Robert tried to focus back on the lecture but he couldn't. He could only think about Stan and how beautiful he was. Robert remembered his offer that Stan was going to be in the library later and he wasn't sure. He just wasn't sure.

As much as Robert wanted to talk to someone, he didn't want to inflict it all on Stan. Stan seemed like a nice, hot, perfect guy, he probably had all the men chasing after him and he didn't need Robert.

He hoped that wasn't true but Robert knew he was just making up an excuse not to go to the library. Granted he actually did need to go to the library to check out a few books he needed.

But he didn't want to do it if Stan was there.

Breathing in more of the perfume in the air, Robert remembered a very hurtful thing that his father (not dad. He didn't have a dad as far as he was concerned) had said again and again.

You must produce an heir to the family name.

Robert frowned as he remembered that saying and how hard and harshly his father had banged it into him ever since he was born.

And that was the real problem.

Watching the slides of the lectures change to show different cells and nerves, Robert realised that that was why his father would never accept him for being gay. Robert had to produce an heir for the family name.

Robert shook his head as he wondered about how stupid it was, so what if there wasn't a biological heir to the family name? Robert might have kids, him and his boyfriend might adopt, foster or go through surrogacy.

He knew he was going to be a great dad, he was great with kids and he was going to be a far better dad than his was. If his kids wanted to be a movie star, gay, straight, trans, whatever. That would be okay. Because Robert was going to love them, be there for them and support them no matter what.

Because that's what a good dad does.

A good dad doesn't force their child into a narrow path in life all because they want a child. And the only true way to get an heir is to have sex with a woman.

Robert realised his face was bright red and sweat was dripping down his back and wetting his neck. Sure he was annoyed but he needed to think about it and most importantly he needed to talk to someone.

Robert didn't like his parents for getting rid of all of his gay friends, his past boyfriends and anyone who could remotely corrupt their son and not deliver an heir. He couldn't believe his father had said gays are wrong because they can't have kids.

But as Robert looked across the lecture theatre, he stared at the staggering beauty, sapphire eyes and tall slim body of Stan. And Robert knew what he was going to do.

He was going to go to the library, talk about his

life with another gay person and live the life he wanted to live. His parents couldn't control him, how he felt or what we wanted.

And right now, Robert really, really wanted Stan.

***

Tucking the rough fabric chair in under himself, Stan smelt the amazing scents of bitter coffee, sweet cakes and citrusy oranges as he sat in the library café at a small two-person table as he waited for the most beautiful man he had ever seen to show up.

Stan looked around the busy café that was between the two massive halves of the library that was separated by a little glass door with lots of tables and students who were drinking, talking and laughing with each other.

Everyone was having a great time, a wonderful time, a perfect time.

But there was still no sign of Robert.

Stan felt his stomach tense as he wondered if Robert would show up. What if Robert didn't want to talk to him? What if Robert wasn't interested? What if Robert wasn't gay?

His eyes widened a little as Stan felt so silly for not even considering that. Stan almost wanted the ground to swallow him up as he wondered if Robert was actually straight and Stan had just made a massive fool of himself.

Then he breathed in more of the bitter coffee scented air.

Stan tried to just relax and enjoy the little break

away from the lectures before he went to his final one of the day. A part of him wondered if the final lecture (Human Sexuality) was some kind of plan from the universe to tell him to have a bit more faith.

But it didn't help.

Stan's stomach still felt tight and his palms were sweaty as he really wanted, needed Robert to turn up. He wanted to help him, he wanted to comfort Robert, he wanted to be with Robert.

Stan still wondered why he was acting like this, he never acted like a schoolboy who was head over heels in love before. But this time he felt different, he was different.

As much as Stan wanted to forget his feelings and focus on listening to Robert with whatever hardship he wanted to talk about, Stan couldn't. He couldn't forget how he felt, the things he wanted to say and do with Robert.

The sound of the glass café door opening made Stan turn around and his mouth dropped a little as he stared at the seductive bright green eyes, strong jawline and longish blond hair of Robert.

He was just beautiful. Stan didn't need any other words to describe him, he was just perfect the way he was.

Standing up Stan looked into those seductive eyes and Robert stared back, they both smiled and walked up to each other. They hugged.

And Stan loved the feeling of the pure chemistry and passion between them.

In that moment, Stan knew Robert was gay and he did care about him, and whatever happened today, Stan knew he was going to stay around, support him and be there for Robert for a very, very long time.

LOVE IN THE WAIT

Sitting back in the hard wooden chair Noah bit his lip as he felt the coldness pulse through him. He hadn't been expecting that but on that cold winter's evening with the snow falling outside, he supposed he should have.

Noah moved himself on the chair as he tried to get comfortable and smiled at across the large wooden table over to the two amazing people opposite him.

He loved his grandparents.

Noah looked at his perfect grandma who was a stereotypical little old lady who shuffled along, tapping everyone's arm as she spoke to them, but Noah really did love her.

Tonight his grandma was wearing her pearl necklace, golden dress and bright red glasses. Noah had to admit she had no fashion sense but she was amazing.

His grandma smiled at him before rubbing her

hands together. Noah had no idea why she was always cold, but she was. He had no doubt she would have preferred to wear a thick fur coat inside the restaurant.

Looking around Noah had to admit this was a beautiful small restaurant with its white walls, wooden furniture and big fireplace. There was something perfectly homely about it and after all the travel back from London, this is exactly what Noah needed.

With the air smelling of amazing meats, cheeses and spices, Noah knew this was going to be a great dinner with delicious food and great company.

The sounds of people talking, laughing and taking orders sounded great to Noah after the hours of city traffic and a silent train on the way home.

Turning his attention back to his table, Noah smiled at his grandad with his full face, straight grey hair and posh shirt. Noah wasn't sure why his grandad always had to look perfect and like he was going to church but he supposed that was a generation thing.

As his grandparents picked up the thin paper menus, Noah just looked at them for a few more seconds. He really had missed everyone since he left for London and work.

Noah really loved his job as an insurance investigator for a large multinational firm with some offices in London, but it never felt like home.

He had grown up in the south east and lived his entire life here. He loved all the (semi-) famous places, like canterbury, Rochester and Dover as they were always fun, interesting and his friends were there.

But unlike lots of other people, Noah had a soft spot for the less well known places in the south east of England, like Rochester, Maidstone and Cuxton. Each of them had their own special things that made Noah love them.

Yet when he was in London, he didn't get to see or experience any of it. He had his own apartment with Westminster and all the great attractions just a few minutes away on the Tube. But it wasn't the same.

Noah used to love London, he loved the London Eye, museums and history of it. But he always felt as if it had been lacking something. Maybe a soul, a community or maybe just something so Noah could call it home.

He didn't know, not really.

But as he sat on the wooden chair and looked at his grandparents, he knew this was home. For home was always where his family and love were.

"Noah how's that job of yours going?" his grandad said, his voice aged but refined.

Noah looked around for a waiter but there were none, for Noah knew exactly where this conversation was going.

"Great thanks grandad. I'm currently working with some investigators on a major fraud case,"

Noah smiled at his grandma as she leant in

closer.

"O that sounds grand No," She said tapping his arm.

"I'm happy for you, but you know I said John's leaving my old company. He has and there's opening for you,"

Noah rolled his eyes. As much as he loved his grandad, he had a terrible flaw of thinking that he knew what was best for everyone, and if they didn't do it then they were silly.

Noah really didn't want to work for his grandad's old company, he used to work as a truck driver in the early part of his life and moved into power stations later on. Noah had no interest in working in a power station, especially a coal one.

"Come on Noah, it is a great job. And John says there's at least two of your kind for you,"

Noah placed one hand on his forehead as he laughed a little. He knew lots of people would have mistaken his grandad for saying *two of your kind* and considering his grandad went to church A LOT, Noah couldn't blame them. But Noah had learnt that his grandad was thankfully fine with gays but sometimes his language did push things a little far even for Noah.

"Grandad I love you and thank you for the offer. But I have said more than enough times, no. And I don't need to work in a particular place to find another gay,"

His grandad nodded and smiled. "Do you have a

boyfriend then?"

Noah tried not to laugh as he saw his grandma lean closer again and place her hand on Noah's arm.

"No," Noah said feeling his face warm up.

"Then this job would be good for you. You'll be closer to us," his grandad said.

Noah almost opened his mouth but he couldn't argue with that and he knew that's what this was truly about. His grandparents just wanted to see him more, and he couldn't blame them. Noah's parents were busy working and at the weekends were spent him with each other, his brother and Noah went he went back. His parents focused on family time but sometimes Noah did feel like they abandoned his grandparents a bit.

Hearing the sounds of other people talking, laughing and enjoying themselves, Noah knew he just needed to steer the conversation another way, but even if he failed that he knew this was going to be a magical evening.

He just didn't know entirely why.

***

Oscar knew lots of people didn't like waiting and working at restaurants, but he did. He absolutely loved it. He got to meet and work with amazing people, customers and see the occasional hot guy as he worked.

And he needed the money. As much as he loved finishing university a few months ago, Oscar wasn't impressed the universities he applied to for his

Masters were taking so long to get back to him. And as Oscar's parents had told him lovingly the problem with a psychology degree was it was useless without a Masters degree at the minimum.

So he needed to work.

Grabbing a warm plate of delicious seafood, peppers and rice, Oscar stepped through the large black doors and entered the main restaurant area.

Oscar always loved the homeliness of it, he loved the white walls that were filled with art, local pictures and fake animal heads. There was something comforting about it all and Oscar loved that feeling.

He started to walk through the restaurant, smiling to the customers and admiring the cute wooden tables. Oscar liked seeing everyone enjoying themselves, in a way it made him feel good about himself. It meant him and his friends were doing a good job.

But he was surprised to see it was so busy in here tonight. Almost every table was full of laughing, talking and smiling customers. That was like a job well done in itself, it meant Oscar and his friends had been doing such a good job that news about how great the restaurant was had spread.

Breathing in all the amazing scents of the meats, fish and spices in the air Oscar kept smiling as he served the customers their food, asked if they were enjoying themselves and checked if they needed any more service.

They didn't.

He didn't know why but for some reason Oscar always felt a bit disappointed if the customer didn't need anything else. Oscar supposed he had been doing waiting for so long, especially at university, that he had always been used to serving people.

Oscar tried his best to keep his smile under control as he remembered how his waiting job had been useful with his past boyfriends.

Pushing those thoughts quickly away, Oscar left the table, walked around the restaurant and checked on more customers.

After a while, Oscar felt his feet ache and pulse tiny amounts of pain up his leg, he knew he shouldn't have worn new shoes to work. That was silly, being a waiter was bad enough after a twelve hour shift with all the standing up and walking.

But using the twelve hours to break in new shoes. That was silly, and now Oscar was paying the price, but in some effort to show he was a professional (or as professional as waiters can get), he kept smiling and serving his customers.

Oscar turned a corner in the restaurant, smiling and greeting the happy customers sitting on the wooden chairs and out of the corner of his eye, Oscar saw someone waving.

He looked at the waving person and-

Oscar was glad he wasn't holding food or drinks because they would be on the floor right now.

Oscar looked straight at the utterly beautiful waving person. He couldn't believe how this stunning guy walked into the restaurant without any of the waitresses saying anything.

This guy was beautiful.

Oscar couldn't stop staring at his strong muscles hiding under a freshly pressed white shirt. That was enough to send Oscar over the edge. But Oscar kept staring at the guy's blond curtain style hair, his strong cheekbones and his eyes.

Oscar couldn't focus on anything but those sparkling eyes that was only made better by the light of the restaurant.

This guy was perfection.

Then it dawned on Oscar that the beautiful waving guy was still waving at him. Oscar didn't hesitate (again) about going to see him.

Oscar *had* to see him.

***

Noah was more than pleased the conversation had changed from his grandad's old company to his grandma's gardening club. It was something Noah was actually interested in, he used to love helping his grandma in the garden as a child, and he had had a few boyfriends that did horticulture at university.

With his grandad on his phone doing God knows what, Noah kept looking at staring at his beautiful grandma with her golden dress, pearl necklace and bright red glasses staring back at him. Noah loved listening to her.

It was even better than breathing in all the heavenly smells of the freshly cooked meat, fish and fruity desserts in the air. This really was a perfect night.

"So I told the judges that my sunflower was taller than Julie's. They agreed and I got first place in the gardening club," his grandma said.

"What did Julie say?"

"O No, Julie wasn't happy. She grabbed the church's wine and poured it into my sunflower. Now it's gone purple and it's growing better than ever,"

Noah smiled at that, trust his grandma to have some strange story for him. He was looking forward to seeing everyone tomorrow, he loved coming home to his parents and brother and Noah felt like this was the first of a lot of great dinners with him returning for the Christmas break.

Noah was never going to complain that as he was a junior, the company felt it was in his interest to partake in the two week Christmas shutdown and let the more experienced investigators continue with the case.

Or as Noah heard it: *we'll give you a two week full pay break.*

After a few more moments of his grandma telling him another story about one of her churchy groups, Noah saw his grandad looking around for a waiter.

"Decided what you're having Grandad?" Noah asked.

"Yes. I always have the lobster in here. It's great. But I cannot find a waiter,"

Noah looked around and saw a waiter talking to

some customers, but he looked done with them now so Noah waved his arm at him. He knew he could be rude but if Noah had learnt anything, it was sometimes you needed to make yourself known to people. Otherwise-

That waiter was hot!

Noah's mind went blank as he stared at the hottie waiter starting to walk over to them, but then the hottie stopped and stared back. Noah was sure if his mind was working he would question that but this waiter was way too hot to think properly.

He didn't know what it was with this hottie that he loved so much, but Noah knew it had something to do with those tight black jeans, big poofy blond hair and fit body.

Normally Noah never thought of guys as fit or hot. It always took him a while to like a guy before he realised he was attracted to them but this waiter… Noah didn't know. There was just something about him.

With the huffing and puffing of his grandad making Noah snap back to reality, he waved the hottie over again and couldn't help but smile as he came over.

He looked amazing.

With the hottie being closer now, Noah stared past that amazing poofy hair, perfect face and his brilliant eyes. He was beyond Noah's wildest dreams, and that was when Noah wanted to kick himself.

He never ever acted like this before, he was a

strong, confident man who didn't think of people as a hottie or beyond his wildest dreams. But Noah didn't know why but for some reason Hottie made him feel weak and so, so vulnerable.

But Noah liked the feeling.

Then he noticed his grandma tapping on his arm.

"Your order No?" she said.

"Huh?" Noah said, snapping back to reality. Staring into Hottie's amazing eyes.

"Your order sir," Hottie said, his voice even more perfect than his face and body.

Noah looked at the menu and picked something random. He didn't want to look away from Hottie for too long.

"Chicken Curry please," Noah said smiling.

As Hottie relayed the order, Noah kept staring at Hottie the entire time. He knew it probably looked weird but Noah didn't care. Hottie was too beautiful not to look at and considering he was probably never going to see Hottie again… Noah wanted to make this time count.

"Anything else?" Hottie asked.

Whilst his grandma and grandad said *no thank you*, Noah was so tempted to ask for this guy's phone number but he knew that wasn't right. At least with his grandparents there and of course Hottie was at work.

Noah shook his head when Hottie looked at him and Noah watched him walk away.

Then his grandma ruined the moment by tapping

on his arm.

"He's definitely one of yours," his grandad said. "Did you see that hair. Oh no, our people don't have hair like that. He's definitely yours and you can keep him,"

Noah smiled at that. He wouldn't mind keeping Hottie.

"No," his grandma said, tapping his arm. "You okay? You awfully quiet,"

Noah blinked a few times and turned to face his grandparents who were both smiling at him. A part of him expected his grandma to smile but he wasn't so sure about his grandad.

"No, you like him?" his grandma asked.

Noah felt his face warm up.

"I did say he was one of yours. You might as well keep him,"

Noah cocked his head a little at his grandad. He was trying to understand if his grandad was just talking or somehow (and slightly homophobically) giving him permission to ask Hottie out.

"Oh Grandad," his grandma said. (Noah never understand why his grandma called her husband Grandad in front of him). "You're telling him wrong,"

Noah straightened his head and smiled at his grandma.

"No, we fine with your people. You have no interest in doing that stuff. We prefer the Church. But we know love when we see it,"

"We've been married for 50 years. Your people might not get that long but still," his Grandad added.

"You want me to go and ask the Hottie, I mean guy out?" Noah asked.

His grandparents looked at each other, a bit unsure and they both looked at him again.

"As long as you promise, No, never to come to church and tell people we encouraged this," his grandma said.

"Believe me. I can do that,"

"Then go. You're young, have fun," his grandma said.

"Even if it is with your own people,"

Noah laughed a little, kissed his grandma's hand and left off into the restaurant. He had to find Hottie and ask him out.

He at least had to try.

***

After giving the order of Waving Guy and his grandparents to the kitchen, Oscar went back out around the restaurant checking on customers and breathing in the amazing scents of meats, fish and rich desserts.

Oscar really did love his job and after seeing Waving Guy, he couldn't believe how great he felt. He wanted to think about why he did but he was enjoying the feeling too much, he loved the way Waving Guy looked at him with his blond curtain style hair and muscles.

He looked amazing.

As Oscar checked with a few more customers as they ate their delicious food at their wood tables, he listened to the chiming of forks against plates, talking and laughing as the night progressed.

Wondering around the restaurant, Oscar hoped no one needed him as he just wanted to look busy and think about Waving Guy. He was so beautiful and it bugged Oscar why he was so fixated on him.

Oscar had seen other good looking guys before and he had always managed to act professionally. But then he realised this guy wasn't good looking, he was beautiful, and Oscar realised he had never used that word to describe a man before.

"Excuse me,"

Oscar turned around to see who said that and he couldn't help but smile as he stared into those brilliant eyes, blond curtain styled hair and muscles of Waving Guy.

With him standing so close to Oscar, he savoured in Waving Guy's strong expensive aftershave and made Oscar feel weak. Oscar wanted so badly in that moment to run his fingers through the Guy's hair.

But then he saw another waiter pass and Oscar remembered he needed to act professionally. He was at work after all.

"Yes sir," Oscar said.

The Waving Guy seemed a little nervous and a part of Oscar dreaded what he wanted to come next.

"I was wondering what time your shift finished,"

It wasn't the exact wording Oscar had planned but he liked it, and he wished more than anything he could just finish work right now and go off with this handsome, beautiful stranger.

But he was at work.

What would his boss say if he found out? What if his boss got mad? What if the other waiters and waitress hated him for it?

Oscar started to feel little drops of sweat roll down his back as he panicked about it. He needed this job for university, he had to save the money, he had to-

"My name's Noah,"

Oscar's mind kicked back into normal gear at the sound of such a beautiful name. *Noah.* Oscar didn't know any Noahs but the name sounded good, perfect for such a beautiful man.

"Oscar," he said.

Oscar loved the way Noah seemed to smile and relax at the sound of his name. Did he like it as much as Oscar loved his? He started to feel hot under the collar and wished his body would behave (in more ways than one).

"What time does your shift end?... If you're interested of course. You don't have to. Actually I'm just going to leave," Noah said.

Oscar smiled as he watched his large strong man get so flushed and embarrassed over him. No one had ever done that for him before.

"Wait," Oscar said. "I get off in about an hour.

Go back to your grandparents. Meet me in the car park if you want to grab a drink,"

Noah smiled at that and Oscar watched him turn away and walk away.

When the guy left, Oscar felt a wave of panic wash over him, he didn't know what he had just done. He couldn't do that. He couldn't grab a drink with a stranger. He-

The passing of a waitress reminded Oscar that he was working and he continued to walk round the restaurant, talking to customers and serving them.

But he avoided Noah's part of the restaurant.

It didn't take long for Oscar to realise he didn't want to go for a drink. He wanted to go home. He wasn't interested in dating. Especially not a stranger he met at work.

He didn't want that.

But he was so beautiful.

Oscar stopped as he remembered Noah's amazing brilliant eyes, blond curtain styled hair and great body. He was beautiful and he was so kind and confident.

As Oscar walked on, he knew he was going to meet Noah at the end of his shift, he was scared and he knew he had nothing to be worried about.

Noah was a great hot guy that Oscar wanted, even if it was for just a drink.

***

Waving his grandparents good bye as they drove out onto the main road, Noah smiled as he remembered how both of them had made him promise to text them when he got home, call them in the morning and tell them all the details.

As he stood there in the small pitch black car park, breathing in the amazing meat scented air, Noah felt a wave of nervousness wash over him. He was nervous for the first time in ages.

Noah knew he shouldn't be. He was always so confident at work, able to handle any situation and handle anyone with a unique kind of confidence and coldness.

But Noah was so nervous.

Despite the cold, Noah's palms were sweaty and he felt wave after wave of nervousness come over him.

He wasn't even sure if Oscar (that was such a hot name!) was even going to show up. Noah still felt bad for basically hunting him down at his place of work, asking him out so he didn't have a choice and running away.

Noah hoped Oscar didn't think of him as a coward or something worse. (Granted he didn't know what was worse than a coward)

But as Noah heard the wooden door to the restaurant open and someone walk out, Noah turned around and smiled. Oscar was standing there.

And all either one of them could do was stare into each other's eyes, Noah loved Oscar's amazing brilliant eyes, poofy blond hair and slim body. He was stunningly perfect.

Then Oscar started to walk over to him and Noah couldn't help himself but walk over to and smile.

They both briefly stopped in front of each other, Noah knew this was awkward but he went in for a hug and Oscar kissed him. Noah loved the taste of his soft lips.

In that moment, Noah knew this was going to be an amazing evening. He had had dinner with the grandparents he loved and now Noah was going to have drinks with a beautiful man.

And Noah hoped drinks would turn into something else. Something that would last a long, long time.

WEDDING, GUESTS AND LOVE

Stepping into the massive white rectangular tent, Jack let his mouth drop as he breathed in the scents of all the expensive perfumes, aftershaves and amazing food. He knew his best friend Octavia would go all out for her wedding reception but this… this was something else.

Taking a few more steps into the warm tent, Jack stared at the massive array of food laid out on one side of the tent. All the little desserts, sausages and other posh nibbles looked marvellous.

Jack looked at the other side of the tent to see breath taking ice statues of swans, (hot) naked men and more expensive things that only Octavia would ever want at her wedding.

Listening to the live band playing wedding music for now on the far side of the tent, Jack knew this was going to be quite a night. Granted he wouldn't expect Octavia to not do all this with her money, she was born in the high life and she definitely lived it.

As Jack returned his attention to the early guests who were slowly walking round the tent admiring the expensive things (and probably wished they had them), Jack felt a wave of unease wash over him.

Unlike Octavia, Jack wasn't born in the high life of the London Elites and he was sure Octavia once mentioned she was some distant relative to some English Lord. Instead Jack was born in the southeast to a middle-class office worker and an engineer so to say he felt out of place here was an understatement.

But Octavia wanted him here.

Noticing the music was changing to become something you could actually dance to, Jack's eyes narrowed on the stream of young men that started to turn up and he couldn't help but smile. Some of them were good looking and attractive, but they all had young women attached to their arms.

Jack was starting to think Octavia had lied about their being gay people to meet here.

It was why Jack was a bit hesitant to come in the first place, he had heard comments of her posh first-class friends about the improperness of gays, so Jack wasn't comfortable here alone. He had wanted to bring his boyfriend along to support him, but then Jack found him in bed with an older man.

So that wasn't happening!

Starting to walk over to the impressive layout of miniature food, Jack felt a small arm wrap around his and as much as he wished it was a hot guy that would make him feel welcome here, he knew it was Octavia.

He gave her a quick kiss on the cheek and looked at her in her beautiful white dress, white shoes and golden necklace.

Jack knew exactly why he had found her attractive when he was straight and they had tried things together. They both laughed whenever they spoke about it as it was that *trying* that made Jack realise he was as gay as they come in the sex department.

Pushing those thoughts away, Jack let Octavia guide him over to the food table and he turn to him.

"Wasn't my wedding wonderful? Did you see the doves, diamond statues and oh my, my husband… now that suit might have cost £2000 but it was worth it,"

Jack took a moment to think of an answer that he didn't make him sound judgemental because, come on, £2000 for a suit that husband of hers was going to wear once. It was a waste of money!

Then he remembered Octavia loved him no matter what.

"Yea, I mean yes. He looked good in it but £2000 really?" Jack said.

"Oh Jacky, you know you can speak common. Sorry, normal with me. And I could never spend that much money, that's what parents are for,"

Jack didn't know if his parents had that sort of money, but it would be great if they did.

"Are you enjoying yourself?" Octavia asked. "Where my posh snobs nice to you?"

Jack had to be honest here. "Why did you sit me next to those old snobs with the purple penguin suits?"

Octavia took a moment to think about it. Jack also didn't know who had a seating plan for the actual wedding part of the ceremony, wedding reception fine fair enough, but the wedding ceremony?

"Oh those snobs. They are a nightmare I'll give you that darling but they're harmless. Why?"

"Because they moved away from me, gave me the dirtiest looks ever and called me a dirty plague, as soon as I mentioned I'm single and I didn't want them to hook me up with any girls,"

Octavia nodded. "O. I remember who you're talking about now. They're all like that here. Snobs are snobs,"

"You said they'll be gay people here who would make me feel comfortable,"

Octavia looked around. "More like gay person but he's great. My hubby Peter knows him, Leo is wonderful. You'll love him I'm sure,"

The sound of someone doing a girly excited scream made Octavia rush off and hug someone. Leaving Jack to wish his parents, friends or work would call him and save him.

But he doubted that was ever going to happen, so Jack really, really hoped this Leo guy was as nice as Octavia said.

***

Walking along the gravelled road that led up to the massive white tent with music coming out of it, Leo felt sweat drip off his forehead as he knew exactly what was going to happen.

Peter (bless his heart) would throw him with some random guy that he would be forced to spend the evening with. Leo would have to do lots of fake laughs, bad jokes and watch the clock tick down to leaving time.

Apparently his guy was great and a best friend of Octavia's but Leo wasn't sure if that was good or bad news. As much as he loved Octavia and he was thrilled Peter had found someone, the other guys she had suggested for him were never good.

Leo smiled as he remembered the last guy. A beautiful muscular guy who was cocky as hell, posh and really dominant. All because he was from money and Leo was not. Leo didn't like guys like that.

As he continued to walk, listening to the gravel crunch under his feet and breathing in the piney scents in the air, Leo hoped this blind date (because it was in all but name) was going to be good.

In all honesty, Leo wouldn't have minded if it was great, amazing even. His luck with men hadn't been the best of late, it was always one bad date after another and Leo just wanted to stop trying.

But he wanted to make one final attempt.

As he got closer to the tent, Leo listened to the great music that only a live band could produce and

Leo took a deep breath before he went inside.

He knew he must have looked like a deer in headlights as he tried to understand everything in the tent. There were tons of people in black and white suits dancing poshly with their plus ones, a massive range of ice statues and a long table full of food.

From his years of going to these parties and posh things, Leo had learnt that all the normal people go to the food table and the posh snobs gravitate towards the wine bar.

Leo looked around for it for a few seconds before he nodded and saw Octavia and Peter had cleverly placed the wine bar near the ice statues, far away from the food table.

Leo had to admit the wife and groom might be posh and over-the-top but they did care about normal people, and made sure they had a safe place too.

As Leo glided through the crowd, breathing in their posh, expensive aftershaves and perfumes, he saw lots of great looking guys but he didn't see anyone of them alone. It probably would have been good if Peter had given a picture of this *Jack* guy.

But Leo supposed he was going to have to find him by himself.

When he got to the food table, Leo stared at all the amazing miniature desserts, sausages and other food that looked stunning. He didn't want to think about much it cost but he was definitely going to enjoy it.

(He might even take it home for tomorrow's

breakfast)

Leo felt someone tap on his shoulder.

Rolling his eyes Leo turned around, knowing this was so typical of the snobby posh idiots here, if someone was in their way then they were inferior to them. Leo was going to tell differently and-

Leo's mouth dropped a little as he stared at the Tapping Man in front of him. He couldn't believe he was about to moan at someone so beautiful (a word he didn't use often). Leo just stared at Tapping Man's bright sparkling eyes, short brown hair parted to the right and his broad but lean shoulders.

This Tapping Man was beautiful.

He knew he had to say something but he felt so weak and strange that he didn't know what to say. He didn't even know why he felt weak, light and strange.

All he could do was stare into Tapping Man's sparkling eyes.

Then it hit him. Leo smiled even more as he realise this was *Jack*. Now he knew he was in trouble- in a very, very good way.

***

After trying to talk to a range of different snobs, Jack decided that they weren't worth his time, he had already been here for an hour and he was already tired of talking about economics, the so-called dangers of the left-wing and how commoners aren't grateful for what the rich do for them.

It was probably after the tenth and *that Labour party will ruin the country* that Jack had grown tired of

the political talk, he couldn't care less about how these posh idiots believed different political parties would ruin their riches.

Jack was happily standing in the corner of the large white tent by the food table and hoped someone would save him soon. He didn't want to be here anymore and he knew as the night went on, the single women would start asking him out.

He had never thought of himself as overly attractive but he was shocked that at every party he went to, all the women asked him out at one point or another. If he was straight, Jack knew he could probably be vastly rich but he thankfully wasn't.

Breathing in the amazing scents of the fruity desserts, meaty sausages and all the other strange food on the table, Jack picked up a small purple tart and ate it.

Jack couldn't believe the explosion of intense raspberry flavour that filled his mouth. It tasted amazing, perfect and just… he needed Octavia to get him some of these.

Jack reached for another one and picked it up… but he dropped it the second he saw *Leo*.

At least he hoped it was Leo.

Jack didn't even bother trying to find his tart again, he was too transfixed at stunning Leo. The way his longish black hair was parted and covered half his forehead was just perfect, his black hair framed his dark brown eyes perfectly and his suit…

In some desperate effort to stop the wayward

parts of his body acting up, Jack forced himself not to look at that stunning Leo in his tight black suit that highlighted all the right places.

As much as Jack wanted to kick himself for wanting to say this, Leo was honestly the most beautiful man he had ever seen.

The sound of Octavia's laugh reminded Jack if he didn't talk to Leo at some point, Octavia would introduce them and that would just be awful, embarrassing and a mood killer for sure.

Jack took a step closer to Leo and stopped. He felt his stomach fill with butterflies, his palms went sweaty and his head went light. He wasn't sure he wanted to talk to Leo.

Then Jack mentally kicked himself, he had to talk to this stunning man, he just had to bring up the courage to do it.

Jack walked up to Leo, tapped him on the shoulder and felt bad about it. He wasn't sure about disturbing people and tapping, come on, who does that. Where were his manners?

When Leo turned around, Jack couldn't help but smile, admire that beautiful longish hair and stare into those dark eyes. Eyes he would happily get lost in.

After a few moments Jack wondered if Leo was staring at him too. Then Jack started to panic and wondered why wasn't Leo speaking? Had he disturbed him? Why wasn't he speaking to Leo?

Taking a deep breath of the amazingly scented air, Jack failed to relax his smile and he spoke to Leo.

"Hi, no um sorry, hello I'm Jack,"

Leo laughed, little lines appeared around his eyes and Jack could see the white of his teeth. He didn't know if he was being mocked or not.

"I'm Leo,"

Jack shook his hand. immediately feeling weak and wishing the handshake would never end.

Leo's smile deepened.

"You like this," he said gesturing to all the posh snobs in the tent.

"No, I'm too common and weird for them,"

Leo took a step closer. "I think I'm going to like you. Should we annoy some snobs?"

Jack smiled and stared into Leo's dark eyes even more, he loved his hot guy's mischievousness and he was definitely a man after Jack's own heart.

The sound of someone tapping a wine glass made everyone turn to the centre of the tent to see Octavia in her stunning white dress standing there. Peter stood behind her.

To his surprise Octavia stared at Jack and winked at him. For some reason he felt like he had been played and Octavia wanted him here to cause a little mischief and annoy some snobs. That sounded like her, and it sounded like great fun.

***

With all the perfectly dressed snobs in the white tent going quiet, standing there and staring at Octavia, Leo took the chance and stared at Jack in all his beauty.

Leo still couldn't believe he hadn't met this stunning man before with his sparkling eyes and beautiful short hair. He was perfect.

The smell of amazing meats, little sausages and desserts filled the air as the coldness of the night started to set in. Leo grabbed Jack's hand out of instinct and went to pull it away but Jack squeezed it and smiled.

Leo was surprised, he wasn't sure what to do. He hadn't done this before in public, he had always saved being gay for behind closed doors but Leo smiled at the idea of annoying people.

A part of him knew it wasn't actually annoying, it was just two men being who they were and if these old posh snobs didn't like it then Leo didn't want any of them in his life.

But he wanted Jack.

The sound of Octavia and Peter starting the normal wedding speech of how grateful they were for people for coming, the wonderful gifts and ceremony made Leo glad Jack was with him.

For too long had Leo not enjoyed these parties and forced himself to date and not be himself in front of his *friends*, but he didn't want that now.

He was tired of Peter and Octavia being the only people who knew the real him, he wanted to share being gay with someone else, whilst still being friends with all these snobs.

Then he realised that all his past relationships and dates weren't awful and failed because of them, it was mainly his fault. Leo remembered how they wanted to go to these parties, work occasions and met Leo's other friends. But he didn't allow that, they grew a part and the attractive guys left.

It was his fault.

Yet as he held Jack' smooth hands, he knew for a fact he didn't want to hide anymore. This felt right, perfect and what he was meant to be.

He didn't care what other people thought, believed or said. He knew what he felt for Jack and nothing was going to change that.

Leo squeezed Jack's hand and kissed him on the cheek. Before realising Octavia and Peter was pointing at them, and there was a massive gasp of shock at them.

Leo looked into Jack's sparkling eyes and saw plenty of lines around them. Jack was happy, Leo was more than happy.

He kissed Jack again.

***

Breathing in Leo's amazing aftershave and feeling his soft lips against his, Jack couldn't stop smiling as they broke the kiss and stared at the rest of the massive white tent.

Jack almost laughed as he saw everyone had taken at least three steps away from them, making most people press against the white material of the tent, the long food table and the ice statues.

Yet Octavia and Peter didn't move, they were both smiling and they raised their glasses at them, and it clicked, it finally clicked.

With everyone silent with only the sound of the cold nightly breeze blowing through, Jack knew Octavia and Peter were doing what they always did.

Scheming.

It was what they loved, a hobby and their job but this time they didn't do it for kicks (mainly), Jack knew they did it because they cared about him and Leo, and they wanted both of them to be happy and in love.

As Jack turned his attention to Leo's brilliant dark eyes, he knew they were right and he never wanted this moment to end. Jack brushed Leo's perfect hair that covered half his forehead away.

Jack wanted to say something to Leo, something romantic, sweet, perfect for the moment, but his palms were all sweaty and his head felt light. He was definitely in love and he knew Leo was too.

They both kissed each other again and the sound of applause filled the tent as this wasn't a celebration of Octavia's wedding, it was a celebration of love.

And Jack hoped this love and moment would never end.

About the author:

Connor Whiteley is the author of over 40 books in the sci-fi fantasy, romance, nonfiction psychology and books for writer's genre.

He is a passionate warhammer 40,000 reader, psychology student and author.

Who narrates his own audiobooks and he hosts The Psychology World Podcast.

All whilst studying Psychology at the University of Kent, England.

Also, he was a former Explorer Scout where he gave a speech to the Maltese President in August 2018 and he attended Prince Charles' 70th Birthday Party at Buckingham Palace in May 2018.

Plus, he is a self-confessed coffee lover!

<u>Gay Romance Short Stories:</u>

Round The Parks and Beyond

Heart Around the Stones

Memorable Night

Love in Halls

The One That Got Away

Gay Romance Collection

Love In The Ingreditents

Party, Love, Christmas

Love In The Wait

Gay, Love, Heir

Wedding, Guests and Love

Gay Romance Collection Volume 2

Keep up to date with exclusive deals on Connor Whiteley's Books, as well as the latest news about new releases and so much more!

Sign up for the Grab a Book and Chill Monthly newsletter, and you'll get one **FREE** ebook just for signing up: Agents of The Emperor Collection.

Sign Up Now!

https://dl.bookfunnel.com/f4p5xkprbk

OTHER SHORT STORIES BY CONNOR WHITELEY

Blade of The Emperor
Arbiter's Truth
The Bloodied Rose
Asmodia's Wrath
Heart of A Killer
Emissary of Blood
Computation of Battle
Old One's Wrath
Puppets and Masters
Ship of Plague
Interrogation
Sacrifice of the Soul
Heart of The Flesheater
Heart of The Regent
Heart of The Standing
Feline of The Lost
Heart of The Story
The Family Mailing Affair
Defining Criminality
The Martian Affair
A Cheating Affair
The Little Café Affair
Mountain of Death
Prisoner's Fight
Claws of Death
Bitter Air
Honey Hunt

Blade On A Train
City of Fire
Awaiting Death
Poison In The Candy Cane
Christmas Innocence
You Better Watch Out
Christmas Theft
Trouble In Christmas
Smell of The Lake
Problem In A Car
Theft, Past and Team

Other books by Connor Whiteley:

The Fireheart Fantasy Series

Heart of Fire
Heart of Lies
Heart of Prophecy
Heart of Bones
Heart of Fate

City of Assassins (Urban Fantasy)

City of Death

Agents of The Emperor

Return of The Ancient Ones

The Garro Series- Fantasy/Sci-fi

GARRO: GALAXY'S END
GARRO: RISE OF THE ORDER
GARRO: END TIMES

GARRO: SHORT STORIES
GARRO: COLLECTION
GARRO: HERESY
GARRO: FAITHLESS
GARRO: DESTROYER OF WORLDS
GARRO: COLLECTIONS BOOK 4-6
GARRO: MISTRESS OF BLOOD
GARRO: BEACON OF HOPE
GARRO: END OF DAYS

Winter Series- Fantasy Trilogy Books
WINTER'S COMING
WINTER'S HUNT
WINTER'S REVENGE
WINTER'S DISSENSION

Miscellaneous:
RETURN
FREEDOM
SALVATION

Printed in Great Britain
by Amazon